Journal of a Schoolyard Bully:

CYBERBULLY

Also by Farley Katz

Journal of a Schoolyard Bully

Journal of a Schoolyard Bully:
CYBERBULLY

Farley Katz

St. Martin's Griffin

New York

JOURNAL OF A SCHOOLYARD BULLY: CYBERBULLY. Copyright © 2012 by Farley Katz. All rights reserved. Printed in the United States of America.
For information, address St. Martin's Press, 175 Fifth Avenue, New York, N.Y. 10010.

www.stmartins.com

ISBN 978-0-312-60658-9

First Edition: September 2012

Printed in July 2012 in the United States of America by RR Donnelley, Harrisonburg, Virginia

10 9 8 7 6 5 4 3 2 1

Bully's Log.
Sunday. 19:00
For my crimes of bullying classmates, torturing lame
teachers, and being a general all-around "bad apple"
(read: awesome boss), the powers that be sentenced
me to go to school in this horrible reform academy.

Mom gave me this journal to—gag—record my thoughts.
I thought about hollowing it out to hide candy or
weapons in, but I think instead I'll use it to plan a
way out of this hellhole. If this is the place I die,
it will serve as a record of the last thoughts of the
world's greatest bully.

Monday

There is a God and he must be a bully, or, at the very least, he's sympathetic to our cause.

Because, for the past three months, it hasn't been easy being Niko Kayler. I've been trapped in the worst reform school in the world—a horrible nightmarish prison where despite being a world-class bully myself, I am surrounded by a phalanx of monsters. Creatures who call themselves bullies but who are in fact just crazed savages. But today, good fortune came in the form of a phone call.

Mom's company gave her a promotion to upper-mid-level managing consultant or something, and the new office is states away in Colorado! I don't know much about Colorado, but I do know this: They don't know jack about me.

I'll start with a clean slate.

I'll be completely free to reinvent myself as I see fit.

And best of all, I won't be surrounded by these fiends at the reform school.

Tuesday

For the past three months, the other "bullies" at this school have been doing nothing but torturing me. Here's a quick rundown of the worst offenders.

KYLE DIGGS

Specialties: Kyle is an old-fashioned bully, who, like bullies from the 50s, prefers a very straightforward beat-down to almost anything else.
Worst offense: One morning Kyle punched me so hard I thought I heard a rib crack. Luckily, it was just the bag of Cheetos I always keep for emergencies in my pocket. Needless to say, the Cheetos were ruined.

JESUS JIMENEZ

Specialties: Despite his massive size, Jesus is not as physically aggressive as you may think. When it comes to hurting, Jesus prefers to go the emotional route, by calling names or by publicly pointing out embarrassing things about you.
Worst offense: During gym class, Jesus astutely noted that "Niko is so fat his butt has its own zip code." With the new more specific nine-digit zip codes, I guess he is technically correct.

Niko's Butt
129 South Back Street
Boulder, CO
80301-2122

MADISON McNULTY

Specialties: Due to a combination of her innate craziness and the massive number of pills she takes, "Mad Madison McNutly" doesn't really have any M.O. other than cuckoo nuts. Worst offense: This probably needs more explanation, but she once snorted a pigeon.

JOSH HIGGINS

Specialties: Seeing as Josh is twenty-nine and a grandpa, his bullying is a bit different from your average reform academy student. When bullying, Josh uses out-of-date references to insult, many of which I don't understand.

Worst offense: Josh ate my lunch in front of me, explaining, "This is for Ronald Reagan and the California Raisins!" I think he is on a lot of the same pills Madison takes.

BRITTANY FLOWERS

Specialties: the school's most innocent-looking student, Brittany is also the most dangerous and the most twisted.

Worst offense: where do I begin? I'll just list three things I saw Brittany do last week.

4

1. After sneaking into the school over the weekend and secretly shaving the school's mascot, Alice the Repentance Alpaca, she brought the shavings to school and forced Madison to eat them.

2. She always carries a Ziploc full of glass shards labeled "Presents."

3. During science class, she used a Bunsen burner to heat up my chair. I haven't been able to sit straight since.   Just look at this butt welt!

To see the unblurred version, you'll have to purchase the NC-17 Director's Cut of my Journal.

This aggression will not stand, man. I'm leaving the state at the end of the week, and before I do, I'm going to get each and every one of these thugs back for the months of pain they've inflicted. I know revenge is a dish best served cold, but I'm too hungry to wait.

Punishment

Just desserts

Retribution

Thursday

I'm going to have to think carefully about how to get these jerks. Bullies are like superheroes—we're powerful and righteous—but we all have a weakness. I just have to find these bullies' kryptonite.

Maybe if I focus on their strengths...

Hmm...or what if I played each of them against each other...

Perhaps constructing some kind of mechanized anti-bully device would...

Only kidding—I just blasted them with a fire hose full of guacamole.

It was pure joy watching those wannabe bullies fall into a giant pit of old guacamole—and not the delicious kind—the oxidized brown kind that smells like dog hospital.

If you're wondering where I got my hands on a fire hose full of guacamole, I know a guy who works at the Taco Tent.

Thursday

If you think those maniacs I sent into the slimy guac-hole were out for revenge today, you'd be right. Unfortunately for them, I would not be around for them to exact that revenge upon. You see, I saved up two months' worth of couch change and paid off a kid at the school newspaper to run a slightly less than real news story.

Reform Academy Reporter

NIKO KAYLER KILLED IN GUAC BLAST-ING INCIDENT. DEFINITELY NOT REPSONSIBLE FOR SAID INCIDENT

And just as extra insurance that they wouldn't trace the crime back to me, I left them a little something I dug up at the local pet cemetery.

HELLO MY NAME IS Niko's skeleton

Never underestimate the stupidity of bullies (except for me). While a high percentage of bullies are what doctors like to call "dumb," I assure you I am far from it. That reminds me, this book is not only a journal, but also a study in the art of the bully, and I've been meaning to add this entry for some time now.

History's Smartest Bullies

Any good study of what it means to be a bully will have to include certain nerdy things like "history," to fully comprehend and appreciate the bully trailblazers, to learn from them and their mistakes, and to make myself a more efficient nerd-intimidating machine.

STEGOSAURUS
Even though T. rex was the most brazen bully in dinosaur times, stegosaurus was

the smartest. Stegosaurus had two brains, one in his coconut, and one in his cocobutt. He also made the wise choice to lay low and watch the T. rex take all the heat for being the jerkiest dinosaur. Then, when the other dinos were least expecting it—BAM!—stegosaurus spike tail to the dino groin. His only mistake was going extinct.

ISAAC NEWTON

This dude was constantly pummeling people with apples. He said he was just proving a point about gravity, but we all know he was in it for the yucks.

LEONARDO Da VINCI

Just look at this awesome dork-torture machine he designed.

CHARLES DARWIN

JK, this guy was a total snot-sack. Opposite of a bully.

JANE GOODALL

This lady was so smart, she realized that rather than waste her time trying to bully human nerds, she could just go live in the jungle with a bunch of chimps and trick the crud out of them all day. Exploding bananas, the "I got your nose" trick, even just shaving the monkeys in their sleep—Goodall was constantly socking it to our hairy little cousins.

BENJAMIN FRANKLIN

This guy was so smart he was constantly inventing stuff to keep the nerd in his place: Bifocals so nerds can easily be identified, libraries to keep the nerds occupied and placated while the bullies rise to dominance, and, of course, the lightning rod, which would later be used to invent tasers for cops to tase nerds with.

THE TERMINATOR

Isn't the smartest human a computer? Yes, if the terminators taught us anything. These future robots were such awesome bullies that they not only terminated nerds, but all human beings. I guess their fatal flaw was not being able to tell the difference.

Friday

Moving day is finally here! The last time I'll ever be in this city full of bad memories! I'm off to a new state and a clean slate. So long, crud-ton! Adiós ciudad del crapo!

> Au revoir la ville de farts!

Saturday

Being stuck in a car with my mom and little brother, Alex, for eight hours a day is misery! Although it has provided me with a captive audience for some road-trip bully techniques I'd been meaning to test out.

1. Throw crap in your mom's hair. Classic choices include spit-wads, chewed-up gumballs, bits of refuse, twigs, and what-not, and the old standby, bugs. Some kids will tell you nothing clutters up Mom's hair quite like a knee scab, but honestly, that's a little crass.

2. Play "I spy," with subtly disguised insults directed at your family.

3. Don't limit yourself to your fellow passengers; use signs to mess with the other folks on the road.

Or use the universal sign that God gave you.

4. Stare out your brother's window. This sounds kinda harmless, but trust me, it works.

Mom got us to quiet down by threatening to drive the car into a ditch. Not to worry, though, Mom's not a real bully at heart. She may talk a big game, but I'm willing to bet that if push came to shove, she wouldn't murder us all just to make a point. You have to have a cold, hard, black bully heart for that kind of outing.

Anyway, by far and away, the best road-trip bully tactic I tried out happened completely by accident when Alex left his cell phone in the car on a bathroom break. He'd been texting on the thing the entire trip, so I decided to send a few texts of my own. See if you can spot where I took over!

5. Acquire cell phone, send terrible texts to other person's friends.

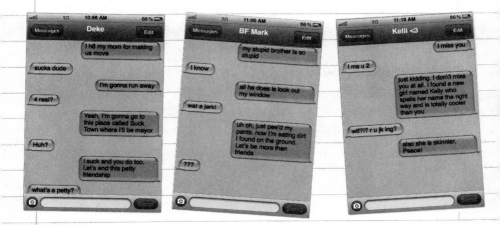

Amazing. I think I've found my true calling. I was able to destroy two friendships and a relationship (isn't Alex too young for that sort of thing?) in under a minute! And the best part is, it was a victimless crime. Sort of.

I don't really get what he's so upset about. Even though I didn't really have any friends back home, who would want them anyway? Friends are just enemies you haven't met yet.

Sunday

We're almost to Boulder and my new life as a free man. Thank goodness there isn't a federal registry for convicted bullies!

Name:
Kayler, Niko
Registered Bully Offender since:
03/14/2003
Offense:
1st degree aggravated bullying of a minor under fourteen (two counts)

Other than the already mentioned road-trip pranks, the car ride has been pretty uneventful, except I did get to see a lot of the majesty of nature or whatever. Turns out nature contains a number of truly impressive bullies.

BLUE JAY

These birds have been known to attack cats ten times their size for no reason. One time, I heard a blue jay got all cranked up on hummingbird nectar and ate a dog.

MOTHER BEAR

Driving through a national park, I saw this crazy mother bear charge a group of tourists. I know she was just protecting her family (lame), but she was also attacking tourists (swag).

MOOSE

I saw this giant moose on the side of the highway. It looked like a jacked-up baseball steroid version of a deer. It was awesome. It slammed its face into a tree just because it could. If this guy were a person, he'd be Mike Tyson (before the unpleasantness).

TRUCKSTOP TRUCKER

I included this guy because it was pretty hard to tell whether he was a man or an animal. A fine line, no doubt. Whatever he was, he sure was good at pushing people around. Amateur-level bully stuff, but still worth a mention.

Monday!

We finally made it to our new home and a fresh start in Colorado. I don't even think I'm gonna miss anyone from back home. Alex said he's going to miss seeing Dad, but you know what—that guy doesn't miss me, so why should I miss him? I made this drawing to reflect how I feel about the subject:

That's all I have to say about that.

Tomorrow is my first day of school at the Organic School for Local Children. I don't want to mess this up—you only get to make one first impression, and how many clean slates do you get in a lifetime anyway? I wonder just what the eighth grade will hold for me. Hopefully, a whole lotta this:

Tuesday

Well, there's good news and there's bad news.

The good news is, the Organic School for Local
Children seems pretty great. It's a very laid-back
environment full of hippie teachers and goofy kids
who love learning for the sake of learning. There's
not a bully in sight. I've got the whole place to
myself. I feel like a goldfish whose masters have
gone out of town and just put an entire week's
worth of food for him in the bowl. I want to eat
it all right now, but I don't want to risk exploding.

The kids I did meet today had no idea what I
actually am! It's like some weird pristine nerd
preserve that has never been exposed to bullies!

Then I met with the principal, Dr. Linda Garrett.
Don't get the wrong idea, just because she's a
doctor, doesn't mean she dresses in a lab coat.
She was one of the grungiest hippies I've seen
this side of
Burning Man.

"Welcome to the Organic School, pull up a bean bag and make yourselves whole."

"Thank you. I'm Mary, and this is my son, Niko. We're so glad you let us enroll this late into the school year."

"Oh, no problem, Niko looks like a real cool kid, and here at the Organic School, we have a saying: 'rules are meant to be bent, friend.'"

"That's great—it seems you maintain a relaxed environment here, but I'm worried Niko needs more structure."

"We don't believe in rules and structure here. Kids are free to learn and grow at their own pace, just like plants and animals in Mother Nature's conservatory that we call 'Earth.' We don't even have detention."

Oh. My. God. Jackpot! After hearing this, I immediately called my stockbroker.

But then came the bad news.

"No detention, no rules... except for the one..."

"Here at the Organic School for Local Children, we have a zero-tolerance policy on bullying. We do not, under any circumstances, in any way, shape, or form, tolerate the slightest aggressive action from one student to another. If you should be caught bullying, even using the n-word—"
"N-word?"
"Nerd...ugh, it disgusts me just to utter it...but if you should be caught participating in any kind of behavior that could be seen as mean or rude, that will be the end of your time here at the Organic School."
"Gulp."
"What's more, we'll write a recommendation to all the other schools in Boulder, advising them that said student is a ruthless bully, a shark in children's clothing, and recommend against enrollment anywhere else throughout the state. Bullying is a worse crime than genocide."
"No more clean slate?"

"Adiós! But, that won't be a problem, will it, Niko? I mean, you don't look like the aggressive type. You're a cool dude, right friend?"

"Oh...yes...coolest dude in town square."

"Great, then we have nothing to worry about. Have an organic day!"

And just like that, all my dreams and hopes of turning the school into an internment camp for nerds, one that I rule with an iron fist, vanished. Poof! Gone.

I don't know what I'm going to do. I have these urges inside of me—to destroy and demolish and noogie—but I have to suppress them. I don't even know if it's possible for me to be a good, "normal" kid. I tried that before and all it did was get me thrown into a maximum-security reform school.

Even the school's mascot is begging to be bullied. His name is "Francis the Free-Range Vegan Chicken," and I think he's a little touched in the head.

But I can't! I can't even eat that stupid chicken! What will become of me?

Wednesday

Two days in here at Hippie University, and it's already becoming clear who the biggest nerd players are. Here's a quick rundown, including some cruel nicknames I'm workshopping. Remember, one of the first steps of being a successful bully is devising a cutting nickname catchy enough to stick.

TERRELL PARKER

Terrell is the worst kind of teacher's pet—he's constantly raising his hand to answer teacher's questions and gain approval—like a caffeinated shih tzu who can't stop yapping for treats. Sometimes if the teacher isn't asking any questions, Terrell will ask a question that is clearly just a disguised way of showing off what he knows. Once he said, "Is it true that the Roman monarchy fell in 508 BC when the Republic was created and the Tarquinian conspiracy formed?" Every class has one of these guys.

Possible nicknames: Lap Dog, Mr. Answers, That-Guy-in-Class-Everybody-Hates

DAFNE UNGER

Due to some crazy tooth-alignment issue, Dafne's entire head is encased in metal. The really aggravating part is that she uses her headgear as an excuse to SCREAM EVERYTHING THAT SHE SAYS! IT'S LIKE SHE IS CONSTANTLY PISSED OFF

AT EVERYONE IN THE WORLD! I'm sure she's faking it, and no one at this prissy school has the guts to put her in check. Just give me five minutes and a magnet and I'll get to the bottom of it.

Nicknames: Loud Mouth, Dr. Screamo, CAPSLOCK

EVAN NGUYEN

Evan has been the school district's valedictorian seven years running (he only lost his kindergarten year on a technicality over who drew the best triangle). His greatest claim to fame is that he is the state's undefeated trivia champion. Word on the street is that he has memorized most of Wikipedia and ninety percent of the stubs! This guy thinks he's so smart. I guess he is, but that still doesn't mean I wouldn't like to encase him in Carbonite.

Nicknames: The Brain, Valejerktorian, Trivia-loser-guy (needs work)

SERENA PEÑA

Serena is fine, I guess, for a girl nerd. It seems like she studies a lot, and she definitely has full-blown cooties. I will say that her voice is sweeter than a thousand candy bars swimming in an Olympic pool of caramel sauce. That still doesn't mean she's not on my hit list.

Nicknames: n/a

RICO TAYLOR

This guy freaks me out. He's like a bizarro-world me if I lost my nerve and bought into the whole studying fad. This is probably the kind of play-it-straight kid my dad would love, so I already hate this guy.

Nicknames: Fatty, Crappy Me, Fatter Me

Also, I guess this guy isn't really a nerd, but I figured I'd include him here anyway:

LARRY THE JANITOR

Shhhhh...

If you ask me, Larry has a touch of the nutzo sickness. He's always pulling me aside between classes and telling me secrets about the government and stuff while viscous ooze leaks from his ears. I guess most people never listen to him, but I know what it's like to be an outsider, so I do. That and it never hurts to be best friends with a psycho.

Thursday

This is really tough. The nerds at this school are the purest I've ever seen, like freshly fallen nerd powder snow on geek mountain. They've been raised in this crazy sheltered world where no one hurts anyone else and everything is happy and made of cotton candy. Haven't they ever watched <u>Shark Week</u>? Don't they know that, sometimes, awful things happen to kind people?

During class I sometimes find myself grinding my teeth and sweating, just staring at these perfect nerds and fantasizing about my triumph over them.

But then I'm snapped back into reality. This school represents my one shot at a new life. I already ruined things for myself back home, but I was given a second chance. Can I possibly change my ways and reinvent myself here?

Ugh! The thought makes me shudder. I don't know how much longer I can hold out before the inner bully makes himself known.

Friday

I think Mom could tell all the temptation at school was stressing me out, so she set up an appointment with some new psychiatrist. I was wary at first, but then I remembered how much fun it was messing with my last shrink. Plus, I really did feel a meltdown coming, and I better talk to someone before this bomb goes off.

BEEP. BEEP. BEEP. BEEP

Evacuate the city! This core is imploding!

Sunday

Just got back from meeting my new shrink, who was a dead ringer for my old talk-doc, Dr. Shaeffer.

"Oh my God, Dr. Shaeffer, what are you doing here?!?!"
"I'm Dr. Shatner."
"Well, if you are, you're the guy's exact clone!"
"No, I'm not."
"Well, are you a nerd and do you have insecurities about yourself and dealings with women?"
"..."
"I knew it!"

Dr. Shatner didn't seem to like that introduction very much, but just like Dr. Shaeffer, he sucked it up and moved on, like a sad little sea sponge.

"So, your mother says you're feeling anxious and stressed out?"
"Totally. I'm at this new school surrounded by the juiciest, most delicious wimps and wieners I've ever seen."

"I don't follow. Elaborate."

"I feel like I want to...you know...bully them. Shame them and make them cry in a public forum, or fire some punches and jam some kicks down their butts."

"Why would you want to do that?"

"Look, Shatner. Let's cut the crap. I know we have doctor-patient secrecy code—"

"Doctor-patient confidentiality."

"Yeah, well, whatever it is, it means you can't rat me out to the feds, so here's the meat of it—I'm a bad kid. I like to hurt and maim and expel the sadness I feel inside outward on those weaker than me."

"That's very observant of you."

"This ain't my first psychotherapy rodeo. Also your shoes are untied."

"Oh, thank you."

"Anyway, Shaeffer—"

"Shatner. Dr. Shatner."

"Whatever. I need your help, because I like this new town and this new school. I've been given a second chance and I don't want to screw it up. I need you to help me figure out how to control myself so that old hippie lady doesn't blackball me from every school in a hundred miles. Maybe you could even help me to make some friends."

"In that case, I think I can help."

Monday

Dr. Shatner told me that I should bring this journal to school and make a list of "triggers" that might drive me to act out and bully again. That way I can catch myself before I "use," as he says. Shatner likes to call bullying my "drug," and bullying kids "using my drug." Sounds kinda gritty and cool, if you ask me.

So here goes—I'll just jot down things as they happen.

1st Period—Earth Science. Trigger: Terrell Parker just answered the last five questions in a row. They were all about bacteria and he answered them all correctly, some of them before the teacher even finished asking the question. I want to put his head in a waffle iron.

2nd Period—English. What in the name of Dog is a
preposition? All I know is it is a part of speech
that is making me furious. Trigger! Also, I can barely
hear myself think over Dafne Unger SCREAMING out
everything she says. I get it. She's angry at the
world. JOIN THE CLUB. TRIGGER!

3rd Period—P.E. I used to love P.E. At my old school,
we'd play awesome pain games like dodgeball and a
version of basketball with punching. But here, at the
Organic School, they've banned all competitive and
violent games. We spent the entire period "exercising
at our own pace." I can't explain in words how angry
this made me. Actually, I can: "Trigger."

Three, four, five...OK, that's
enough for today. Wouldn't want
to blow out any strength muscles.

4th Period—Algebra. This is my worst subject. Just being in this class makes the blood in my face boil so hot it feels like the skin is melting off. Also, I had a daydream where my dad said I was getting too fat. Double trigger.

5th Period—Lunch. This is my best subject. Thinking about lunch is the only way I make it through the rest of the day. I am a lunch superhero—like some kind of X-Man whose power is eating lunch at a really high level of expertise.

Foodenator—we need your help down at the food factory. Some kids are trapped under a pile of food, and we need you to eat them out!

Unfortunately, I was just about to enjoy my salami and mayo sandwich when a stupid, good-for-nothing butterfly landed on my hand and ruined everything. I hate the beauty of nature! Natural trigger!

Gnarly, man—you're one with nature. Right on.

She left before she could see me eat that stupid, beautiful bug.

6th Period—Reading. I'm the only eighth grader in this class. Reading is supposed to be a seventh grade thing only, but because of my grades at my last school, they made me take it too. Everyone must think I'm a dullard. I don't think I have to explain to you how angry this makes me (trigger-level angry).

7th Period—History. I like history. I'm good at it. History is full of hard-as-granite bullies taking what they want by force. Swords and guns and bombs—it's the best! What I do not like is the looks I got when my chair gave out beneath me.

No one said anything, but I could tell they were all thinking that the chair broke because I am fat. Can I help it if I sometimes eat my feelings? Is it my fault that ice cream is delicious? I've made a list of the witnesses to this horrifying incident. Erase them, erase the incident.

8th Period—Español. No estoy español. Translation:
I hate Spanish. This class usually pisses me off just
because it's the last thing standing between me
and an ocean of snacks and video games at home.
Today, though, all I could do was relive over and
over again the chair incident in my head. What's
worse, it was in Spanish this time.

Things could not get any worse.

Tuesday
Things have gotten significantly worse.

After yesterday's crap storm, I was already feeling
terrible. I was looking forward to coming home
and watching my favorite cartoon, World War VII: Dogs
Versus Cats.

So I flipped on channel 723 to watch the cartoon gore
unfold, only to see that WWVII has been canceled and
replaced with some girl-friendly show called Princess
Flower and the Cupcake Crew.

And then this.

Just as good as candy? Just as GOOD as CANDY?
Well, something snapped, and I went ballistic. I just
wasn't ready for the combination of things that
hit that day. I grabbed the first thing I saw—which
happened to be Alex's prized possession—a two-
foot-tall Transformer model my little brother had
spent countless hours gluing together—and smashed
it into the phone. Alex was less than happy.

At that, I charged the little brat, but he was too quick and slippery. He hid in his room and locked the door. I figured I would just kick the door in, but after a few kicks, it still wouldn't open, so I threw a lamp at it, then I punched it a bunch of times but it still didn't budge.

Mom was not happy when she got home.

Alex was kinda upset too.

I think maybe I pushed him over the edge. Oh well, time for some week-old emergency pizza.

Wednesday

After the little "smashy smashy" incident, Mom
scheduled an emergency session with Dr. Shatner. I
gave him my list of bully triggers from Monday.

"It seems like literally everything makes you
want to bully."
"No, not everything."
"A butterfly made you angry."
"I told you—I hate the beauty of nature."

Shatner said he was worried about me acting out
and hurting myself or others, so he prescribed me
some calm-down pills to mellow me out and make
me focus. Fat chance I'll take those.

He also told me to continue writing down my triggers and angry feelings—that it might help me avoid getting thrown out of school, but then he said that in "all likelihood" that would probably happen anyway. The guy has no faith in me! Then I told him that in all likelihood, he'd end up dying alone, sitting upright in a moldy La-Z-Boy, in a one-room apartment in the bad part of town. I showed him a drawing of the scenario to clarify.

How do I know all this? A simple Google search returns this guy's LiveJournal archive. Old people have no idea how the Internet works—it lasts forever.

Ain't I a stinker?

Also found: while Googling Shatner, I stumbled upon a video he made in college.

Do I really have to do this in my underwear?

It's a student art film—who's gonna see?

File that away for later.

Friday

Before school today, I was thinking more and more that Shatner might be right. The Organic School is just too chock-full of losers and brainiacs ripe for a pounding. I gave myself one week before I slip up and get expelled. But then I went to school and something amazing happened. I heard something I hadn't heard in what seemed like years—the sweet sounds of crying.

Amazing! With a few simple keystrokes, this girl Hillary had reduced her best friend to tears, and without a single shred of evidence left behind. Anyone could have sent that message! This was my epiphany—cyberbullying—a thing I once thought of as the last refuge of wannabe bully poseurs who have to hide behind their computer screens—might be my only chance.

I should have realized cyberbullying's potential on the car ride to Colorado when I first felt its supreme power and lightning-fast effectiveness. I feel like an old geezer for not embracing it sooner.

This will be my salvation. Well, maybe not, but it is truly my only hope for release here at the Organic School for Local Children where even mosquitoes are considered "blood bullies."

I'm no fool—I can't roll into this thing naked. I've got to learn the ways of cyberbullying—learn to leave no trace and how to attack with maximum tear seepage. Say goodbye to old Niko and hello to Niko 2.0.

Sunday

I spent the weekend researching cyberbullying online.
There's so much free info out there on how to be a
jerk! Technology is amazing!

After nearly thirty straight hours of researching
without a break, even for sleep, I heard a terrible
sound from the living room. I went to investigate
and found this monstrosity.

Apparently Mom felt guilty about Alex being so upset
with the move and decided that it would also be
a killer combo punch to me for smashing his stupid
robot statue to go and buy Alex a stupid slobbering
puppy of his very own.

"Jealous" isn't the right word. "Furious" doesn't
quite capture it either. I guess I was "Furjealious."

Monday

A new player is emerging in the bully game (besides yours truly). At first glance it appeared that the Organic School had never been touched by the malicious grip of a bully, but I've started to notice a pattern.

> Can you believe Hillary called me a skank?! Is that like some kind of skunk? What'd I ever do to her?

Her name was familiar from the last teary-eyed girl I'd run into at school. Then this:

> Check out this video Hillary sent.

> Ha ha—look at those nerds. Oh wait, that's us.

It's time I addressed my rival in the cyber war.

HILLARY CORRIGAN

After a little asking around,
Hillary is apparently one of
the "popular girls." When it
comes to boys, bullying just
makes you an outcast, but
apparently girls who bully
other girls get elevated to
the status of GODS. Oddly,
she seems to target mainly
people who view her as a close friend. Perhaps
this is how she keeps herself from getting
ratted out. Even so, something seems out of
place. Why wouldn't one of those computer
lab geeks just turn her in and get her ejected?
Dr. Garrett would jump at the chance to bust
this cyberbully. It would be like her second
Woodstock.
Nicknames: Arch Nemesis, Cyber Rival, Girl Me.

Tuesday

I'm eager to get started cyberbullying, but honestly, I'm terrified of getting caught. It seems like everyone at this school has a cell phone, but I don't. I threw mine into a river when it autocorrected "my bad" to "me fat." I asked Mom for a new one and she just laughed and laughed, and then poured herself a big glass of wine, said "new cell phone," and then laughed some more before drinking the whole glass in one sip! I guess I could use Mom's phone, but if she didn't catch me, Dr. Garrett certainly would. I still can't figure out how Hillary is getting away with it. Still, I'll give her credit where it's due.

Elsewhere...

Girl's got skills.

Thursday

I came home today to find SugarTummy—what a horrible name, BTW. The only name more pathetic than that is Baby Chipmunk or Candy-Face-Choco-Pup. Ugh.

This dog's entire existence is a slap in my face. Alex got him for being a wimp and crying over spilled robots. I've got to teach him a lesson or there will be no justice in the world.

I sat SugarTummy down for some special training lessons before Alex got home from ballet class. I know, don't get me started.

If Alex got this dog for being a wiener, the only just thing to do will be to turn it into his worst nightmare.

No one said this was going to be easy.

Friday

After a long week at school without a single opportunity to cyberbully, I was all pent up with bully rage. Luckily, I had a meeting with Doc Shatner. While in the waiting room I set up the office computer to loop a certain video.

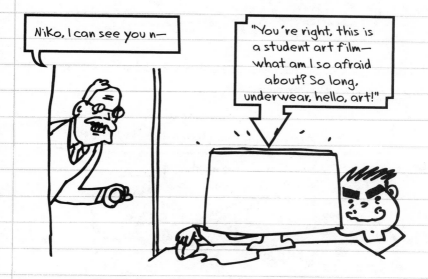

I also added a passcode and locked the computer.

I could get used to this. Bonus—his head nurse was witness to the entire thing.

The best part about an embarrassing Internet video is that it is hilarious and hurts no one.

Saturday

If you have a problem you can't solve, I always say just let your brain marinate on it for a while. Eventually, the answer will come to you. We were driving to the grocery store when the solution to my cyber problem came to me.

I'd needed to convince Mom to go along with my plan.

"Hey, Mom, you know how you're always saying I should get a summer job?"

"Yes, it'll teach you responsibility, give you structure."

"Yeah, that's great—it'll also give me cash to buy phones and stuff."

"Yeah, that too, I guess."

"So do I have your permission to get one now?"

"You can't have a summer job—it's the middle of the school year."

"I know, but I'll just work weekends. I'll have plenty of time for school stuff, I promise!"

"Hmm...I don't know."

"Come on, Mom, what about all that structure and crap like you said?"

"I suppose it couldn't hurt."

"Awesome! Look, Radio Hut is hiring—can we stop in?"

"Niko, I'm impressed with your go-get-em attitude."

"I'll also need some cheeseburgers afterwards. For stomach structure."

The plan worked perfectly. Mom signed off on parental consent as I'm not old enough to work under my own will—once again, China one-ups us!—and I got a part-time weekend job restocking batteries. The manager was a little reluctant to hire me, but he came around when I whispered to him that I'd work for cell phones. He said I could start tomorrow.

The only downside is I have to wear this ridiculous uniform. They only had size XL, which usually fits. I guess I should go easy on the baco-chee-burgers.

Welcome to Radio Hut. Can I interest you in something expensive that will break almost immediately?

Sunday

Just got back from my first day at "the office."
Boy, working is for losers! My boss sucks,
customers are jerks, and after a full day of work,
I only got one disposable cell phone.

The manager, Mr. Chandrasekar, said that I
could hold out for a few more days work and
get a better phone with a bigger screen and a
permanent number, but I realized that might be
traceable. If one day's work earns me a disposable
phone, that's two phones a week I can use to
cyber taunt and then just throw them away—burn
them—without any fear of getting caught. This is
just like <u>Breaking Bad</u>!

On a side note, I saw MurderZombie (aka SugarTummy) chase a cat up a tree today. He's got the taste for blood. Tomorrow his training continues, and my fieldwork at the Organic School begins.

I'm so excited I can barely sleep. This is like Christmas morning but where the presents are other kids' tears!

Monday

Success! My burner phone worked perfectly. After snatching Terrell Parker's phone number from his Facebook, I spent all day texting him threats. Any time he raised his hand to answer a question, he'd get one of these puppies.

BLOCKED NUMBER:

Lower your hand or so help me I will jump out of this phone screen and lower it for you.

At first he was reluctant. The dude seems to love answering questions correctly as much as I love candy and pain infliction. So I had to keep up the pressure.

He got the message. For the rest of science class, the sweet sounds of silence filled the room. When the bell rang, Ms. Biel could tell something was up.

I love impeding education.

Tuesday

One thing that really upsets me about this new school is the physical education program. Hippies should never be in charge of something so specifically designed to pit one kid against the next in a mortal struggle for physical supremacy. The Organic School has completely missed the point of P.E.

So today, I decided to send Coach Price a message. Normally I wouldn't feel the need to sock it to a coach. Most coaches are like adult bullies—tough, angry, they scream and yell so much the veins in their face and neck almost explode. But, like everyone else at this school, Coach Price is a huge peace-hugging tree-lover in need of a wake-up prank. I got his number off a flyer in the teacher's lounge I found before school.

It was obvious that Coach wasn't getting any responses with this hyper-wienery ad, so I was willing to bet he'd jump at the chance of a possible roomie. I was right.

This next game is called Friend Ball. The best part is there's no ball at all, just friends, so everyone wins! Oh, excuse me one minute, I have an incoming electronic textual message I must attend to.

Old people are like giant babies who suffer from depression and anxiety.
Here was the content of our text exchange:

"Hi, is this Coach Price?"
"Yes."
"I'm asking about the room. How much does it cost?"
"$400/month. Interested?"
"Yes. But there's just one thing."
"What?"

"I can't say. You might...judge me...."

"No! No way! Coach Price does not judge anyone. Your background doesn't matter to me."

"Really?"

"Definitely."

"Great, because I'm an ex-con and it's really hard to find a roommate who's cool with that."

"Huh...do you mind if I ask the crime? It was probably some mix-up, right? That kind of stuff happens all the time."

"Nope. Not really a 'mix-up,' so to speak."

"Huh...well, then, it's probably some kind of misdemeanor, right? I once stole a pack of gum by mistake! (When I realized what happened I went back and paid double, just to be safe.)"

"No, nothing like that."

"Was it graffiti? I tend to think that street art is an expression of oneself."

"Sort of. It was murder."

"..."

"Double murder, actually."

"...oh...I see...."

"Yeah, real violent affair. The jury said I killed my two former roommates and then ate them slowly over the following months using only a straw. In prison they called me 'the Milkshake Man.'"

"Huh...well, they probably got the wrong guy, right? Our justice system isn't perfect."

"Nope. I did it. The killings, the eatings, the whole nine."

"...did they...did they hurt you, and you were just defending yourself?"

"No! Kind of the opposite, in fact. They were just too nice to me. I hate it when a roommate is so kind and sweet and all hippie-like. It just makes me want to...want to...SCREAM!!!!!!!!!!!!!!!!!"

"..."

"Anyway, where do you live? I'll bring my stuff by this afternoon."

"..."

"I don't have much, just a bed and a box full of straws. See you soon! MM"

When Coach came back, he was pretty shaken. It looked like he'd just seen a ghost or something. So when I volunteered to teach the class a new game, he was too pale and sweaty to care. He just said he needed to go take an Echinacea and lie down. It was great!

This next game is called Pain Ball. No one is a friend, and everything is a ball. The object is to survive.

Wednesday

Yesterday's prank on Coach Price was so much fun,
I just had to keep it up. I reverse-traced Coach's
cell phone online and got his home address. Then I
sent him this.

"Hey Coach, it's me again (The Milkshake Man).
Listen, do you live at 519 W Newbury?"

"Don't come here!"

"I'll take that as a yes."

"How did you find me?"

"Lucky guess? One more question—how big is your
freezer? Bodies...I mean...food goes bad so quickly—
is it big enough to store say 184 lbs of 'food'?"

"I've called the police and they are coming to my
house now!"

"Oh! Also, are utilities included in the rent? Summer
electricity can really put a dent in the old bank
account."

"Leave! Me! Alone!"

Coach didn't show up for school today. A substitute told us not to be worried, that he was safely in the hands of police protective services. At this point it seemed like a good time to get rid of my cell phone. I'll have to wait till next week to continue the cyber party.

All sins are forgiven in the white hot cleanse of flame.

Also, FYI, I know "burning" a cell phone doesn't mean literally burning it, I just have a thing for fires. Should probably talk to Shatner about that....

Thursday

Every Thursday, Alex has ballet class. This is the neutron bomb of nerdy after-school activities— having him for a brother, it's kinda like if Superman's brother were Lex Luthor or if Bruce Wayne's sister were poor. I've spent hours trying to explain how lame ballet is to Alex, but he doesn't seem to get it.

Don't you see how much of a nerd you are? Ballet is for girls and weird, sweaty dudes named Leslie.

You wouldn't understand.

I even followed him to class once on my bike. I was totally right!

This is the perfect time to train the MurderZombie to become a grizzled junkyard menace, like me. I started with some basics.

When that didn't work, I tried to tap into the hound's more basic instincts.

Oooh, la di da, look at me, I'm a fancy cat from the rich side of town. It would be oh so terrible if some tough, mean dog bit my butt.

Against everything I've been taught by cartoons, this failed too. I had to bring out the big guns.

Are you ready for some gut-wrenching internet videos?!

I forced MurderZombie to watch two straight hours of cute kitten videos. That's enough to drive any kid insane. After this marathon session, the Zombie was showing some positive signs of improvement with the stuffed cat.

It's only a matter of time before MurderZombie is so strong she rises up and eats me and my whole family in our sleep.

Friday

Dr. Shatner was extremely impressed with my progress. Well, I guess I should technically say that he was impressed with the lies about the non-existent progress I lied about. Usually, I don't condone lying unless it is in the service of a larger scheme of deception, but I couldn't just tell Shatner about my cyber life. He's probably so old that he wouldn't even get it.

It was just better for everyone involved if I pacified the situation with a harmless lie.

"You see this, Shatner?"
"What is it?"
"That's my one month bully coin. I have been off bullying for a full thirty days and nights."
"That's fantastic news, Niko! Honestly, I didn't think you had it in you."
"Yeah, I know, you geezer."
"What was that?"
"I said bullying is a disease—like the flu but more awesome and fun—and I just have to take it one day at a time."
"You made some big progress here, Niko. You should be very proud of yourself. And, your mother tells me you've even taken up a part-time job? All without getting in trouble at school."
"It must be those magic calm-down pills you've been giving me."

Yep, the pills have been doing amazing things, as building blocks for this pyramid under my bed.

I'm not a Scientologist—I'm not necessarily against psychiatric medicine, but why alter what's perfect?

Sunday

I spent the entire weekend slaving away at Radio Hut. Seriously, customers are the absolute worst. I'm sitting there, trying to plan out my next move, and some bug-eyed human sweat sock has to come bother me about a part for his broken geek box.

Do you have replacement microphones for this MMORPGs? My team desperately needs me.

You desperately need a shower.

Niko

Usually I just ignore these people by pretending to be deaf and blind, but Mr. Chandrasekar caught me a couple times and told me if I don't help the customers he'll fire me. Ugh.

Anyway, I somehow made it through both shifts.
And that means two phones!

"Are you sure you want to be paid in more
phones? I've got some very nice laser disc players
and yPats around back."
"What's a yPat?"
"It's a Taiwanese knockoff iPad. The display has
six-point-five colors!"
"No, just the phones, please."
"What does a boy your age need with so many
phones anyhow?"
"What's it to you?"

"Well, it's none of my business, but it seems like the kind of people who have many disposable phones are the same kind of people who participate in criminal activity."

"You get that from watching <u>Breaking Bad</u>?"

"Maybe."

"Well, it's none of my business, but it seems like the kind of people who pay fourteen year olds to work in their store by giving them store merchandise might not be in the position to ask so many questions."

"Well played."

"Want to watch <u>Breaking Bad</u>?"

"Yes."

Since our little discussion, Me and Old Man Chandrasekar have been getting along much better.

Work on Sunday flew by, and as a bonus, I came home to find Alex in tears.

Yeah, things were cruising along just fine when Mom got a phone call from Dad. Like always, she yells a lot and slams the phone when she's done.

"I've got bad news, Kids. This was supposed to be your father's weekend with you, but because he's a self-centered egomaniac who thinks the world revolves around him, he decided to take next weekend instead."

"He can't do that!"

"That's what I told him! There are rules, he can't just do as he pleases! But we agreed to compromise. Alex, you'll go with your dad next weekend and Niko will stay here."

"Not fair! What about SugarTummy? I just got her!"

"Don't worry Alex, I'm sure Niko can watch her, right Niko?"

"I can't! I have to restock the batteries with Mr. Chandrasekar!"

"Well, I'm sure he'll understand."

"No! That's not fair! I want to work! It gives me structure or whatever!"

I ran into my room, where I'm writing this now. I don't know what I'm more pissed about—the fact that I have to watch that drooling puppy and possibly endanger my awesome job—or the fact that my dad basically said he loves Alex more than me. He didn't even have to hesitate. The phone call lasted like three seconds and Dad knew he wanted to see <u>Alex</u>. Well, I've got news for Alex —SugarTummy isn't the only one around here who can shred stuff.

Fear is the path to the dark side. Fear leads to anger. Anger leads to hate. Hate leads to suffering.

He's always been the favorite. Does Dad even know about the ballet lessons? I'm just going to store up this anger and release it in a productive way on the dweebs at school this week. Dr. Shatner would be proud.

FYI, I also made a "mess" on the living room carpet.

Monday

I had yet to select a target for my next cyber onslaught by the time I went to seventh period history, a place where I've already embarrassed myself by being so fat that my chair buckled and collapsed under my weight. Luckily none of these Local Kids had enough guts to make any jokes about it, so they live to see another day.

I went to sit down, but forgot to remove my backpack first. I realized immediately that I was stuck in the chair. What can I say—being fat isn't all fun and games. That gives me a great idea for an ironic T-shirt.

Don't judge me—by the year 2020, all Americans will be this big.

Porte-Party

The best option, as far as I could tell, was to sit still and wait for the class to end and the bell to ring. Once everyone emptied out of the classroom, I could then struggle and flail like a dog with its head trapped in the fence until my desk shattered and I was free. However, things did not go according to plan.

Hey, wait, everybody! I think Niko is stuck. As a fellow large-boned individual, I understand this kind of thing. Let's circle up and help him.

I feel bad because that punk Rico Taylor was just trying to help. He's fat too and, like me, has probably been escorted off his share of roller-coaster rides with restraints "unequipped to accommodate someone of our build." The dude probably knows the husky section of the department store like the back of his fat, fat hand. Muffin top? Try muffin tops. In another world, we could be buddies.

But in this world, we are enemies. I could have been in and out of this situation with no problems, but Rico had to stop and point it out for everyone to see. Once the kids started massaging me with oil, I couldn't take it anymore.

Yep, I now know who my next target is.

There was one upside to all this unpleasantness.
I think that my little exploding-out-of-the-chair
stunt may have impressed a few of the kids,
namely Serena Peña.

I'll never wash that muscle again.

BULLY MOVIES

There aren't enough blockbusters out
there where the protagonist is a bully.
Almost every movie in theaters has some
underdog nerd for a hero while the bully
is cast as the villain; either that or it's
just a bunch of zombies running around
screaming. This is ridiculous! Here are five
killer ideas for movies where the bully is
the hero.

THIS CHRISTMAS, DAN HATES
EVERYTHING.

A REAL
Shark's Tale

From the people who brought you heart-warming family movies that end with smiles, comes a gritty, hard-to-watch movie about the sadness of real life.

**FROM THE PRODUCERS OF *NASTY DAN* AND
NASTY DAN II: LIFE SUCKS COMES THIS THING.**

If Hollywood is looking for me, I'll be in my
room, minting more gold with my gold-minting
machine (my brain).

Tuesday

Phase one of Operation Destroy Rico Taylor is in full effect. On a side note, I'm particularly looking forward to this takedown. At least once a day in the hallways, someone mistakes me for Rico.

I had to get to his locker when I was certain he wouldn't be around, so I snuck off during lunch and planted this inside:

Dear Rico,

You have passed first election to the Black Ibis Society, a highly secretive brotherhood of men. Come to the steps of the school library tonight at midnight to await further instructions. Tell no soul and burn this correspondence.

1876.

P.S. If you're still hesitant, this will be good for your college applications or whatever.

Wednesday

I'm pretty exhausted today. Was out late with Rico last night, but I think it'll be worth it.

Sneaking out of the house at night is no easy task. My mom's room is right next to the front door, so that is not an option. I thought maybe I'd keep quiet by using MurderZombie's door to the backyard, but that idea backfired.

After some struggling, I freed myself and climbed
out through the alley and grabbed my bike. I
made sure to leave a decoy in my bed in case
Mom checked in on me.

At the school library I planted one of my burner
phones in an envelope and left it on the library
steps. Lying in wait, I half expected Rico not to
show, but then at exactly 11:59, I heard his fat,
wheezy breath. Punctuality is the calling card
of the chump.

There is no cure for asthma, but with this medication I can significantly reduce my chance of an outbreak. Tell your partner about your asthma.

I used my other phone and dialed him up with a voice-altering box I "borrowed" from Mr. Chandrasekar (relax! I'm returning it this weekend).

"Listen carefully, Embryo. Do you wish to become a full member of the Black Ibis Society?"

"Whoa—your voice is all deep and scary like the man from the movie previews."

"Answer the question! Do you want to become a member of the Society or not?"

"Yes, I think so."

"You THINK so?"

"I'm mean yes, yes I do. Sorry, it's past my bedtime and I get kind of wonky when—"

"Silence! If you wish to grow beyond an embryo into a full member, you will have to demonstrate your humility."

"My humidity?"

"This Friday, you must humiliate yourself in each of your classes."

"Like how?"

"Ugh! Can't you do anything yours—you know how that kid Nico got trapped in his chair yesterday?"

"Yeah, that was sad."

"Well, stuff like that. Really humiliate yourself and call attention to it so everybody sees."

"I don't think I understand."

"Idiot! Look, there's a list of suggested pranks in the envelope. Just pick one for each class and do it, OK?"

"OK, I guess."

"You GUESS?"

"Well, I don't even really know what the Black Robot Society is."

"It's Black IBIS Society, you nitwit, and it's a really cool really awesome secret thing that should be your top priority in joining. Everyone who's anyone is a member—both President Bushes, all your favorite cartoon characters, Obama's uncle—the list goes on and on."

"Oh, OK."

"One last thing."

"What?"

"This is a SECRET society. There can be no evidence."

"Oh. I won't tell anybody."

"No, the list."

"What about it?"

"Sigh. Memorize it and eat it."

Eh, I've eaten weirder things.

Friday is gonna rock my underpants.

Thursday

Another Thursday, another lesson with the MurderZombie. I thought today I'd take him on a field trip.

We're going to the happiest place on Earth! The dog pound!

I figured this could be a kind of reverse Scared Straight thing to show him the potential he has. When we got there I said I was interested in a dog to guard my junkyard. They showed me some pit bulls and rottweilers, nothing out of the ordinary. I knew I was going to have to grease the wheels a little bit.

They took me and the Zombie on a long walk to a holding pen set a full mile back on the property. As we approached this stone prison, the barking got louder and louder until it was almost deafening. MurderZombie peed. I'm not gonna lie, I did a little too.

Twenty yards out, the attendant handed us a Key and said she could go no farther. She made me sign a few waivers, blessed us with holy water, and then sent us on our way.

This pound is a no-kill shelter, so these dogs are
here for life. Inside it was like some twisted mental
hospital for the dogs that society cannot contain.
One dog's chart said that he was incarcerated here
for eating a family of smaller dogs. Another just had
the word "monster" written on it. There was one dog
with two faces, and one who wore a cat skin on his
head like some kind of sick trophy. But at the far end
of the enclosure there was a surprisingly cute little
dog named TreeTop.

All the neighboring dogs seemed frightened of this puppy and I couldn't figure out why. She had the biggest blue eyes, I got lost in them. Staring into those big puppy eyes, something happened to me. I found myself trying to open her padlock. My hands were uncontrollably drawn to her release switch.

Just then the attendant who escorted us there twirled me around and slapped me in the face. "Your eyes are playing tricks on you! That dog has dark powers!" I looked back and what I saw shook me to my core.

Lucky for us, the attendant got us out of there before we became puppy chow. Overall, I'm not entirely sure our little field trip worked as I had hoped—MurderZombie looked more terrified than intrigued—but it did give me a bunch of nightmares that I won't soon forget, so that's a plus.

Friday

I'm pretty thrilled I invented the stupid Black Ibis Society. It has already served me so well. Here is the day's play-by-play.

1st Period—Toward the end of Science class, Ms. Padrick asked if we could name the six naturally occurring noble gases. Rico stood up sheepishly, and farted six times. Between farts he said, "Fartonium, Stinkon, Smelloxygen, Buttripium, Leftoverpizza, and Prffft." The class ate it up and his face turned as red as an apple. He sat down. After class, in typical hippie fashion, Ms. Padrick lectured him on how self-expression was a good thing, but only when done in an appropriate way. She gave him a pat on the head and sent him on his way.

2nd Period—Rico and I aren't in the same second or third period classes, but word of his antics got back to me fast enough. In his geography class, Rico was seen putting on some kind of pig costume and eating a giant can of pig food.

3rd Period—Rico picked some choice gems from my list of humiliations.

4ᵗʰ Period—While wasting away in Algebra, something in the hallway caught my eye.

5ᵗʰ Period—I was already hoping for something great for lunch. The entire 8ᵗʰ grade is gathered in one place and the air was filled with tension. You could tell word had spread that Rico was up to something, and everyone wanted a front-row seat. This is was what it must have felt like at the Roman Colosseum when the gladiators were waiting for the lions. Just then, Rico appeared with a boom box and the cafeteria went silent.

He pushed play for music that I can only describe as hardcore dance club bubble-butt house bouncecore. He proceeded to dance in a style to match.

Look at me. I'm humidifying myself to show my humidity.

The dance led Rico to the serving line and the mashed potato station. In a move that I'm willing to bet converted more than a few girls into future nuns, Rico began to slather himself in the potatoes.

Unfortunately for Rico, he would not get to complete the rest of the day's humiliation stunts. Mr. Loggins nabbed him and gave him over to Dr. Garrett, who sent him home to recover from what she saw as "an episode catalyzed by post-modern urban corrosion from cell phones and computers and whatnot." She gave him some scented homeopathic oils and called his mom.

I was thinking that I would go ahead and make him a member of Black Ibis anyway, for putting so much effort into the five stunts he did complete, but then I had to sit through the rest of the day.

My plan backfired because, somehow, Serena thinks that that four-eyed fake-me oaf is a comedic genius. Those were MY pranks! I designed those feats of humiliation. Serena should love me! On a side note, she smells like a warm glass of cocoa with a sheet of fabric softener in it.

Maybe I could wear glasses tomorrow and pretend to be Rico?

I should punch myself in the stomach for even thinking such a thought.

Sunday
Luckily, I convinced Mom that she should let me work this weekend and that she should watch the dog. All I had to do was turn on the waterworks and she melted.

Please Mommy, I need work! I'm saving up to buy you a nice present!

OK, OK, just keep it together. Sheesh.

What? Bullies aren't above crying to get our way. It's textbook sociopathic behavior.

Mr. Chandrasekar was out this weekend, so I had to watch the store all by myself. It was way easier than I thought it was going to be.

Two more days of "work," two more cell phones.
I'm getting to be an expert at this.

Monday

This Thursday is the statewide trivia competition—
the one that Evan Nguyen has won three years
running. I don't have anything personally against
the guy—we're not in any of the same classes, and I
hardly ever see him anyway, but as a bully, it is my
sworn responsibility to throw a wrench in the gears
of any and all such nerdy behavior. At my old school,
I took it upon myself to ruin each and every science
fair. Since the Organic School doesn't have a science
fair, I'll have to settle for ruining the "Brain Bowl"
trivia competitions.

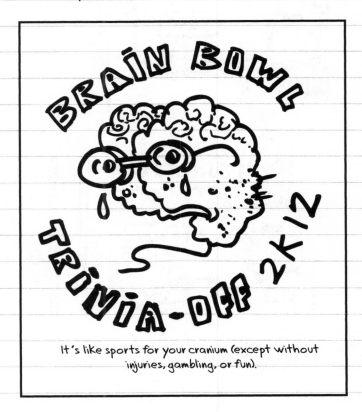

It's like sports for your cranium (except without
injuries, gambling, or fun).

Wednesday

The Brain Bowl will have to wait, because today is the day that dweebs and bullies alike look forward to all year—Halloween! I don't care about crappy costumes or delicious treats—I'm in it for the tricks. You can get away with basically anything on Halloween.

Boys will be boys on Halloween, I suppose.

The last thing I wanted to be doing on Halloween was dying a slow death on Shatner's couch, but Mom had scheduled this appointment a month in advance. I had to figure out a way to get out of it.

Dr. Shatner, is it OK if I wear my costume in the office today? I'm going trick or treating after this and don't have time to change.

Sure, no problem.

Then I let him have it.
As predicted, Shatner rescheduled, making
up some lie about needing to take his kids
trick-or-treating. He doesn't have any kids!
I Facebooked him—his relationship status has
been "single" since the early seventies.

On the way home, I passed the park where I saw
Alex walking MurderZombie. I hid in some bushes and

spied on him.
Little do they know that dog is well on its way to
becoming a bloodthirsty Dog the Ripper. I was about
to run over there and break up the cute festival,
when I got a tap on the back.

They definitely would have understood it was a costume if I hadn't lost my leaf in the bushes. The whole completely naked in a bush thing was enough to make them drive me home to Mom, who wasn't thrilled to see me.

I tried to explain to Mom that she should be happy that this was only the first time the police have had to escort me home, AND that it wasn't for murder or something that would inspire an episode of <u>Law and Order</u>. Anyway, she grounded me for a week, so I guess Halloween pranks are out. Bummer.

Here's what I would have done, if I weren't grounded.

Whatever. It just gives me more time to prepare for this week's cyber attack on the Brain Bowl.

Thursday

Today was the big day. I made sure that this year's Brain Bowl would be one they wouldn't soon forget.

Every good fight needs an audience. While the Romans filled a coliseum to showcase their lions, I have the local news to cover mine. I called a bunch of reporters and told them that the principal was going to give a controversial talk on how all races are equal, except for one. Most of Boulder showed up.

Wow, super cool of so many people to show up for the Brain Bowl. Way to support local, organic kids! I'd just like to take this opportunity to mention a personal choice—I've gone one step beyond Vegan. I'm now Barren, which means that I do not eat anything at all because everything, even rice, has a soul. I encourage you to do the same. Peace.

Because I'm a good sport, I even stopped to wish Evan good luck before he went onstage.

Things started off normally enough. Evan Nguyen was dominating, answering every question with a word-for-word encyclopedic and correct response.

Patiently, I sat there and watched as Evan slowly took down his opponents. I even had the pleasure of sitting next to the headgear and braces surrounding the girl known as Dafne Unger.

After each correct response, I used one of my two new burner phones to text the correct response to the other—a live blog of this historic event. And there's no way Dafne noticed—she can barely see out of that headgear.

It was down to Evan and some nerd from East Central. If I had to guess his name, I'd wager it was "Langston" or maybe "Mummy-face Jerk-juice." After five consecutive rounds of questions, the Bowl went into a sudden-death lightning match. Exciting stuff if it weren't so painfully, soul-crushingly dweeby.

I hate to say I told you so.

Just then a loud cell phone rang out, interrupting the quizmaster from delivering his oh-so-important news. The same phone I had been texting all the correct answers to. The very same phone set only to ring for one specific number. The precise phone I had planted in Evan's pocket an hour earlier when I shook his hand and wished him luck.

As you can imagine, it was pretty hard for Evan to explain why the phone in his pocket had all the correct answers texted to it. Yes, this might be the one trivia question Mr. Know-it-all Showboat Brainiac would not be able to answer.

Success! Now all I needed was a fall guy to finger as the accomplice and complete the picture. But I couldn't turn someone in—it would look too suspicious. Luckily for me, headgear is magnetic.

All it took after that was a casually dropped word in front of the reporters, who were all too eager to make a story. They overheard me talking about how I was sitting next to some braced-out girl texting answers the entire time, and the next thing I knew, it was on the evening news.

An elaborate texting scheme was uncovered today at the state Brain Bowl. The students responsible for the cheating have been suspended. Now for the weather, we'll go to Ugly Jim, who is temporarily replacing Heather, the sexy weather girl, while she undergoes cosmetic surgery. Jim—

Thanks Karen! Oh, it's gonna be real sunny and pretty out. Like really, really pretty, like opposite-of-me level pretty.

And it was.

The only thing sweeter than annihilating your enemies is watching a beautiful local news-caster tell you about it. Also, maybe candy.

ch 4.

Friday

In a few cunning moves, I had successfully vanquished all the major nerd players in the school. Well, maybe not Serena, but I'm working on something extra special for her. She passed me a note in math class today— my heart jumped when I read it.

Not only does Serena have an evil streak— one that wants to cheat—but she also wants to cheat with yours truly! She might be the perfect girl.

Obstacles conquered, enemies bested, Serena
note received, I strutted down the hall like
my butt weighed a million pounds.

Not everyone seemed happy for me. I spotted
Hillary Corrigan giving me the stink eye.

Did she know I was behind the stunt? Or did she resent my awesomeness?

Yes, this is what it feels like to be drunk with power.

Saturday
Even Dr. Shatner noticed how great I was feeling.

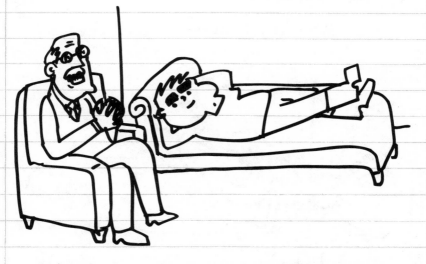

"Niko, you honestly seem really mellow and self-
fulfilled. I'm getting some very positive energy
from you right now. It seems your journaling is
really helping your life view."
"I don't know what you just said, but I do feel
mega sweet."
"Why? What's so 'sweet' about it?"
"I completely destroyed—"

I caught myself before I gave too much away. I know I have doc-patient secrecy or whatever, but I always say never let your doctors know too much about you and the truth, or they'll use it against you.

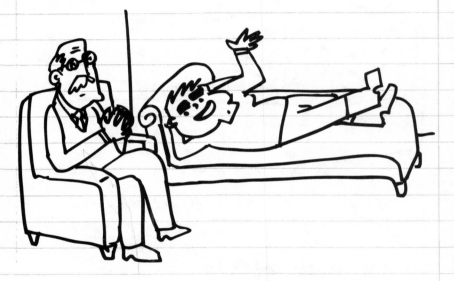

"I completely destroyed my addiction to bullying. I hope. One day at a time. Praise the Lard! Etcetera."
"The Lard?"
"I mean Lord. You know what I'm talking about."

Bullet dodged. And don't think I let Shatner off
the hook that easy. After I wore my costume in
on Halloween, Shatner had the computer removed
from the waiting room and replaced with
antiquated paper magazines. Boring! So I brought
in some of my own books to replace them. I used
the photocopy machine in the teacher's lounge
to make a few dozen flip-books composed of
stills from Shatner's art film.

**STUDENT ART
FILM:
A DIFFERENT TIME**
a graphic flipbook
by Theodore S. Shatner

Contains material inappropriate
for people of any age

I think I heard him scream when I left. Well, it was
more a combination of screaming and crying, like
the sound a horse makes when it explodes of
sadness.

Sunday

I put the finishing touches on my grand plan for the lovely Serena Peña. I can't actually believe I'm about to write these words, but I think I have a "crush" on her. I know—this is nuts. Everything in my brain is telling me that she's a stupid girl and full of crap like flowers and almonds, but I just feel... well, I just like her and want her to like me.

If anyone in a position to hurt me should find this journal, the works and events depicted herein are purely works of fiction and do not connote actual crushes.

All day at Radio Hut I was trying to figure out how I could get Serena to like me. Then it hit me:

INCEPTION.

Mr. Chandrasekar and I were watching a pirated copy
of it. In it—spoiler alert—Leonardo DiCaprio uses a
complicated system of dreams within dreams to dive
deep into the subconscious of others and implant
an idea inside their brain so that they believe this
idea grew organically out of their own mind.

"Hey Mr. C, is it cool if instead of two phones this
week, I just take one and some of this other crap?"
"Yes, but shhh...DiCaprio is totally about to incept
this knucklehead."

"Speaking of, what do you think you'd need to build one of those inception machines?"

"I don't know, just grab a bunch of stuff!"

"What about one of these answering machines, you think that would work?"

"Yes! For the love of—you just made me miss the part where DiCaprio incepts the guy. Great! Now I have to rewind a chapter. I hope you're happy."

While Old Man Chandrasekar was glued to the TV, I helped myself to everything I could fit in my backpack. I'm not exactly sure how to make this work, but I swear on this stack of semi-stolen two-way pagers, that I will *INCEPT* Serena with the idea that she likes me and that I am awesome. And, if there's time, the idea that she should order me a pizza. Incepting builds up an appetite!

Monday

After almost ten hours of construction, my inception machine is finally complete. I even did some trial runs on MurderZombie.

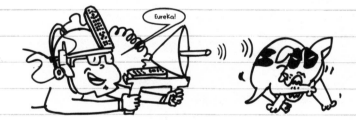

It worked! True—dogs do enjoy chewing their legs anyway, and maybe this was just a coincidence that after using my inceptor ray to implant the message "bite your leg," that's exactly what MurderZombie did. But maybe not. Tomorrow, we find out. Wish me luck, whoever it is that is reading this.

Tuesday
Operation INCEPT SERENA almost hit a snag today.

"What are you doing?"
"Uh, nothing."
"What is that thing on your head?"
"What thing?"
"That helmet."
"Oh, this? This is for math. Because we are in math class. It's a math helmet."
"Uh, OK? What is that ray thing?"
"Math ray."
"You're up to something, Niko Kayler."
"No, I'm not."
"..."
"So, does it work?"
"What?"

"The math ray and the math helmet. If they work, I could really use them. I've gotten nothing but C's in here all year."
"Uh—not sure it works. I'll let you know."
"You're weird."
"No! You are the one who is the weird one person!"
"You're funny."

If that isn't a sign that this incepto ray is working, I don't know what is. Plus, that was literally the longest conversation I've ever had with...well, with any girl...at least where it doesn't end in her running away from me. Does this count as getting to second base? I'm going to have to consult the Internet as to what exactly "second base" is.

Oh. My. God. Child lock! Engage the Child lock! My eyes!

Thursday

I waited all week for another sign that Serena might like me, but nothing conclusive happened. She did touch my shoulder, but I think it was just to slap a fly that had landed there.

Gotcha! Geez—there sure are a lot of flies on you. Ever heard of soap?

Can I help it if my overactive sweat glands and love of foods high in trans fats causes my sweat to be more potent than the average guy? Girls can be so cruel.

This whole operation has gotten me all twisted up inside. I can't think about anything else. I'm full of... what's that stuff called...oh yeah, teenage angst.

I hate everything! Ugh, the world is unfair! I want to listen to loud, screamy music!

I decided I need to put my mind at ease with a little diversion. Luckily, Alex was out balleting it up, so MurderZombie would be available for some advanced combat lessons.

Kill the hippie! Bite him! Eat him! In the police report I'll say that he attacked us. KILL!!!!

No matter how much I screamed "Kill," the dog
just didn't seem to want to do it—I guess the
murderous rage that lives inside of me doesn't
also exist inside of him. Maybe the girl he
loved didn't tell him that he stinks and that
she'll hate his smelly face forever. Even giving
MurderZombie a demonstration with the hippie
scarecrow didn't work.

This is for supporting jam bands!

Today just isn't my day.

Friday

INCEPTION worked! It must have just had a
delayed reaction. Look at this text I got today!

BLOCKED NUMBER

Hey Niko! It's the girl
that you like. Well, I
like you too, and I
want to meet up. Come
meet me this Saturday
behind the football
field by the big oak
tree at 3.

Serena?

Come alone. ;)

I don't even know how she got my number and I
don't care! I like her and she likes me! She gave
me a winking smiley face for crying out loud. That
has got to be at least fifth or sixth base, right?

Mr. Chandrasekar wanted me to work a double, but he'll have to handle it himself. I've got more important things to do.

I wonder why Serena wants me to come alone? I wonder if she's gonna want to make out or worse! I better get tested for cooties after, just to be safe. I'm so excited, I don't think I'll be able to sleep tonight.

Saturday

I showed up to the football field almost an hour early—I didn't want to be late—but I also didn't want to be too early, so I hid in a bush under the bleachers.

Does dot com stand for "dot communist"?

A boy's thoughts tend to wander when squatting in a bush.

At three p.m. sharp I bolted over to the big oak tree behind the field to make sure that Serena could see me there—I didn't want her to miss me. I waited, and I waited. I got a horrible sinking feeling that maybe I was getting stood up. Was this even a date that I could get stood up from? I wanted to puke.

Just then I heard something in the branches above me. It sounded like snickering, and then:

"Haha! Look at the stupid fat chicken who thinks some girl could actually like him."

"What the hell is this? Hillary Corrigan—how did you know I was going to be here?"

"Who do you think sent you that message? Serena Peña? Likely. I saw the way you creep out and drool over her with your sick little love ray or whatever. It's pathetic."

"What is this stuff?"

"Vegan chicken feed is really sticky, isn't it? It's almost like glue. I think you'll find those chicken feathers are pretty hard to get off."

"I am going to destroy you for this."

"Do your worst. You'll just get expelled. There's zero tolerance for bullying at the Organic School. Which brings me to my next point—I'm the cyberbully around here. This is my territory! I own this mother puking school. Don't think I haven't noticed you trying to horn in on my corner. This is a warning shot. You cross me again, and next time it'll be live ammo. Capisce?"

"Well, if I can't destroy you myself, I'm going to turn you in for this. You're not getting away with this—I promise you that."

"Sure I will. I always do. I've been bullying idiots here for years and never get in trouble."

"How do you—"

"My last name may be Corrigan, but my mom's last name is Garrett, as in 'Dr. Garrett.' Hippie ladies don't take a married name."

"I'm still turning you in."

"It's your word against mine, and who do you think she's gonna believe? Her sweet little daughter, or some bloated, smelly sack of chicken feed?"

"..."

"Later, Tubs."

I have never been more debased in my life. I didn't think it could get any worse but then Francis the Free-Range Vegan Chicken strolled by and decided to have a snack.

Sunday
I didn't waste any time today. Mr.
Chandrasekar was watching a marathon
of the Terminator movies, and as bad as I
wanted to watch those robo bullies destroy
the human nerds, I had work to do.

For Radio Hut payment this week, I decided
to take a very specific phone, the bright
pink slide-around that that monster Hillary
Corrigan uses as her primary weapon in the
war on her "friends," and a keyboard.

Planting this phone on Hillary wouldn't be easy. She's going to be expecting me to retaliate—I won't be able to get within a hundred yards of her. This might be tricky. I'm going to need help.

"Hey, Mr. C—do you think you could do me a favor?"
"What? I'm trying to watch the part where the Terminator terminates the guy."
"Could you kidnap this kid and drive her out into the desert, make her dig her own grave, and then just leave her? No actual killing, just, you know, scare her really bad."
"No way! I'm not doing that again."
"Again?"
"I'm trying to watch the Terminators!!"
"Sorry."

Well, that was a blow. I'm still going to need to help, and I think I have a plan.

Wednesday
Sorry for the lack of entries, but I've spent the week gathering intel and planning. Some very important things to note:

Hillary Corrigan's 13th birthday is this coming Monday. If there's ever a good time to strike, it's when someone least expects it. I spent the week acting like a scared puppy any time we passed in the halls so she'll think I'm a broken man, a beat-down animal. That way she'll never expect it when this viper strikes.

Most of the seventh grade—by my estimates, 82 percent—is logged into Facebook all day, every day. They are messaging and chatting each other for more of the day than they are doing school stuff. Amazing.

In addition to ballet, it appears my little bro Alex is also enrolled in a baking class. Dear God, what is wrong with that boy? But this might work to my advantage.

"Hey, listen, duder—do you think you could whip me up a batch of special cupcakes for this coming Monday?"
"Go fart in your own mouth."
"Come on!"
"Seriously—just go leave me alone and go do whatever weird crap it is that you do with all those cell phones."

"You're my brother, and I don't mean that in the urban sense. We are literally flesh and blood! You owe me."

"I don't owe you anything except maybe a punch in the nose. You have never done anything nice to me. You only live to destroy what I love. Leave me alone!!!"

So much for giving Hillary poisoned b-day cupcakes. I guess it's better to stay away from any possible felonies anyway. Back to the bully board.

Thursday

No time to train with MurderZombie today. Plus, I've kind of given up on that stupid dog. She is so cute and sweet it makes me sick! In topical terms, she's a Miley Cyrus when all I want is a drunk Ke$ha.

I needed to make a list of insults and cut-downs for Hillary. I thought this would be no problem, but when I sat down to do it, here's all I could come up with:

You stink! Take a shower, Smelly

You are so fat that your fat has fat

Mr. Tubs

Nobody likes you

No girl could ever like you

I hate you and so does everybody else

After writing these out, I realized these are all insults that Hillary threw at me. I think my mind is too clouded to do this exercise. Usually I would kick butt at this, but I'm going to need help with this one too. I need someone pathetic who has heard a lifetime of insults of every flavor and creed. I think I know just the guy.

Friday
"Shatner, my man!"
"Oh, hello, Niko, how
are—"
"Listen, I've got
this great idea for
some revolutionary
therapy. A kind of
role reversal thing
where I pretend to
be your therapist."
"Huh, sounds interesting, but I'm not sure—"
"Oh, just do it. Here, lie down right there and I'll
sit in your chair. It will give us both great insight
into me or whatever."

It took a little convincing, but soon, I was deep
into the psyche of a tormented and defeated nerd.

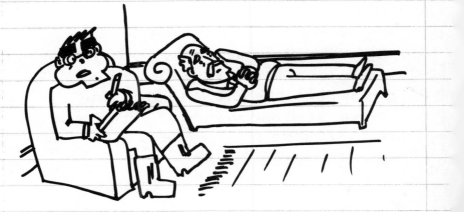

"So what else did the mean kids call you when they wanted to make you cry?"

"Everything! Pee-brain, Professor Jerk, Old-lady Legs, the walking wiener, the suckstronaut."

"Hold on, I have to write these down, they are hilarious!"

"What?"

"Nothing, continue. What other hurtful things did they say to you?"

"They told me I'd never amount to anything, that everyone in school hated me, that girls would never like me, that my own family wanted to get rid of me, and that I am a worthless loser."

"Wow. Tough stuff."

"I've never told anyone these things. It actually feels so good to open up to—"

"I'm afraid that's our time."

There was still plenty of time left, but I'd gotten what I needed from the guy. I now had over two hundred painful insults ready to go.

Saturday

I needed the weekend to prepare and run trials. Monday's attack has to be perfect, because I'll get only one shot at this. I had to practice typing, and timing, and hold an important secret meeting or two. There's no way I'd have time to go into work.

"Hey, Mr. C, it's Niko. Listen, I can't come into work today."

"That's the fifth time you've called in this month!"

"I know, but I have some important stuff to take care of."

"If you don't come in today, don't bother coming in tomorrow."

"Thanks!"

What a nice guy!

Sunday
I just took an ultra-secret meeting with Kimberly Hale. Who's that, you ask? She was actually the first person I met at the Organic School for Local Children. I found her crying in the hallway after her best friend Hillary had ruined her chances with the boy she likes. Typical best friend stuff. If anyone would be willing to help me get back at Hillary, it would be her jilted best friend.

"Thank you for meeting me on such short notice."
"What's with the voice-changer box and disguise? Are you going to kidnap me?"
"No, I just wanted this to be a secret meeting."
"Well, I know who you are, Niko—you don't have to use that thing."

"Oh. How did you know?"

"The whole school knows about what Hillary did to you. They call you 'the fat-range chicken.'"

"Damn. That's pretty good. Listen, I know Hillary has crossed you too."

"Maybe."

"So, maybe you'd want to help me get back at her for these things she has done to us."

"No way! Hillary is my friend."

"Breaking up relationships isn't something that friends do, last I checked."

"I...I...I know! That witch!"

"Does that mean you're in?"

"I'm listening."

On my way home, I stopped at the store and picked up some balloons. You can't have a birthday party without fun balloons.

Monday

The big day. My hands were sore from typing. I was so nervous I couldn't eat anything this morning. Well, technically I had a couple slices of leftover pizza, but compared to my normal fare, that is practically nothing. What? I'm fat. Get over it.

The day's events took careful planning and timing. From watching Hillary over the past week, I'd noticed she has two chunks of down time when I could likely gain access to her phone.

> Seventh period study hall. This had all the hallmarks of a good time to strike at Hillary: An entire hour "supervised" by Coach Price, who, from what I could tell, sleeps through this period along with most of the class. Hillary, however, uses this time to text. I would have no hope getting a hold of her phone during study hall.

> Lunch. This is Hillary's time to shine—her social hour. I don't think she even eats, she just drifts from table to table, making the rounds, and putting down her friends. She usually doesn't even touch her phone for these fifty minutes as she can do all her bullying in person. This would be the window for action.

This would also be the biggest window for a screw-up. I know what I'm capable of, but I had no idea about Kimberly Hale. Would she chicken out? Would she even be able to do what we discussed? I was petrified. The lunch bell rang. I hid behind some lockers at the far end of South Hall. Then I saw it— Hillary Corrigan walking and texting down the hall on her way to lunch. Getting in one last jab at some poor friend, probably telling some popular girl that her dress was too short or not short enough or both.

At the other end of the hallway came Kimberly. She was already late and looked super nervous. If she screwed up now, there'd be enough evidence to get me kicked out or at the very least suspended. But then it happened. Kimberly executed the plan masterfully. Faking an accident, she crashed into Hillary, sending both their phones flying.

In the mix-up, Kimberly successfully grabbed Hillary's phone and left her with my Radio Hut decoy.

With a wink, Kimberly slid me Hill's phone down the hallway. I snatched it up and retreated to the one safe place I had in the school—Larry the Janitor's closet. I guess my willingness to listen to Larry's crazy stories had paid off—he now considers me a friend and lets me use his closet to hide candy, or hang out, or even launch a full-scale cyber attack on the school.

Using Hill's phone, I had access to her texts,
Facebook, Twitter—all logged in and ready to go.
It was time to take my long list of painful insults
from Shatner and send them to every kid in the
school. My fingers being too large to do this
effectively, I had purchased a keyboard.

Initiate Operation Widespread Sadness.

Over the next forty-five minutes, I sent so many
hurtful messages, e-mails, and texts, I must have
set a new record for words per minute. I probably
also racked up a monstrous bill for Hill. I didn't

have time to think, so luckily Shatner's list was there to help. Did you know somebody once called him a "slutty little grandma"? That guy needs more therapy than I do!

After the marathon session, my fingers were like noodles. I had to get the phone back to Kimberly so we could do a trade back. I met her outside the cafeteria, gave her the phone, and put ice on my hands. It was up to Kimberly again, but another "accidental bump" would be too obvious—Hillary would know something was up. That's where the Black Ibis Society came into play.

In addition to my ultra secret-meeting, Sunday also involved some late-night texts with Rico Taylor. He was instructed that as his final, final, final initiation into the Society, he would have to deliver a little birthday present to the birthday girl.

"What the hell are you doing in front of my
locker, fat-for-brains?"
"Hello, Hillary. I have been instructed by your
secret admirer to give you these balloons and
candy for a present."
"How sweet, now get out of my way."
"For the Dark Ibis, Lord of Shadows!"
"What?"
"I said, look at this adorable puppy in
celebration of your birthday."

This was the moment—while Hillary was blinded
by the cuteness of the MurderZombie, Kimberly
slipped in and exchanged the phones. I was so
proud. She put the expert gypsy pickpockets of
Barcelona to shame.

Hillary may have been able to get away with bullying her group of girlfriends, who were too crippled by fear of unpopularity and middle-school obscurity to turn her in, but as soon as my texts circulated through the rest of the school, the tattletales came out of the woodwork. The line of complainers outside Principal Garrett's office was so long she couldn't ignore the problem any longer.

Would Hillary Corrigan please report to the principal's office. Immediately!

I figured Hillary might be able to talk her way out of this one, or maybe just commute her sentence down to some community service, so as insurance, I had one last rabbit in my hat.

Although Hillary couldn't explain how her phone had sent all those nasty messages, even one calling Coach Price a "slutty little grandma," she could certainly try.

"This is so unfair! I can't believe you think I did this!"

"I'm sorry, Hill, but the evidence is overwhelming. If I don't do something, how can I possibly defend our zero-tolerance bullying policy?"

"But I didn't do it—I'm being framed!"

"Hmmm...I suppose that is possible."

"You know who it was—probably that freaky nerd Rico Taylor! He was all weird and came up to me after lunch—he probably snatched the phone from me then! He's the one you want!"
"Do you have any proof?"
"Yes! He gave me these candies. Look!"

I knew Hillary was too concerned with staying skinny to touch those candies, or even check them, and I figured this would be a good opportunity to unload my large supply of calm-down focus pills I'd been pretending to take while stashing under my bed.

"Pills! Drugs! INORGANIC things! Hillary!"

"I swear, they're not mine!"

"How could you! I'd heard about teenagers and drug problems on TV, but I never thought it could happen to my baby!"

"Mom, can't you see? This is all one big setup! Rico gave me the drugs and stole the phone and did the texting!"

"All I can see is a sad little girl under the spell of her pills."

"Mom!"

"Don't Mom me! I'm Principal Dr. Garrett, and you are hereby suspended, pending rehab and counseling!"

"But—"

"I'm calling your father to come pick you up. I'm extremely disappointed in you."

Nico: 1
Everybody Else: Nothing.

I'm back, suckers.

Tuesday

Today was the last day before Thanksgiving
break. I'm actually kind of looking forward to
it. Alex and I are supposed to fly out Thursday
and visit my dad at his new place. I can't
remember the last time I saw him.

Anyway, as the dust cleared from the big cyber
attack, it seemed maybe my plan had worked
a little too well. An assembly was called in the
auditorium.

Because of the recent
cyber attacks perpe-
trated via cell phone,
I'm now instituting a
school-wide ban on all
phones from here on out.

Kids were pretty upset about this. This also means that my days of using burner phones and covert cyber attacks are over. I'll have to spend this Thanksgiving break thinking of a plan. And eating. Mostly eating. Thanksgiving leftovers are the best!

I'll set up camp here for the night and save the rest of you for tomorrow.

Wednesday
The ships have hit the fan.

I just called Mr. Chandrasekar to schedule some hours—I was hoping to barter for some non-cell-phone device that I could use at school, but Mr. Chandrasekar had other things to say.

"Mr. C, it's Niko. Do you have any shifts today?"
"For you? No. I fired you, lazy bones."
"Very funny, when can I come in?"
"How about a quarter past never. You're fired. Deal with it, hombre."

I thought he was just being nice last weekend when he gave me Sunday off too. I guess he fired me.

I had barely hung up when the phone rang again. It wasn't what scientists might call a "good" conversation.

Hey Niko, it's your dad—listen, I'm not going to be able to have you kids out here after all this Thanksgiving. Some work stuff came up and I've got to go see a client last minute. I know you guys will understand. Have a great Thanksgiving, but don't eat too much—nobody likes a guy who eats too much, if you know what I mean. All right. Got to hang up now. Ciao!

Are you kidding me? The man has the audacity to last-minute cancel my Thanksgiving and then call me fat. I'm so angry right now. All my foot and toe knuckles just popped at once. Did you know your eyes could pop? They can.

Thursday

Crappy Thanksgiving! I was feeling like such puke today that I could barely enjoy my three pounds of turkey and patented gravy drink (gravy + soda). Mom could see I was feeling down so I was excused to go eat in my room.

Then I realized something great—I don't need them—I don't need anyone. I don't need Dad, or Mom and Alex, or the kids at school, or even cell phones. The answer to all my problems was right here in front of me all along.

The warm blue glow of the computer screen is all the friends I'll ever need. This dinky little box can connect me to every middle school nerd, dweeb, and doofus cootie-bag in the world!

I spent all day (and night) researching the possibilities, and here's what I found out: they are endless. I feel like until now, I didn't really even know what it was to be a "cyberbully." More soon.

Saturday

Over the past seventy-two hours, I haven't slept. Technically that's enough sleep deprivation to classify me as clinically insane, but to be honest, I've never felt more clarity. I have discovered my true calling, and it is cyberbullying. I've leveled up, as they say in Cyber Town.

CRIMINALLY
INSANE

ABSOLUTE
CLARITY

Since I'm seeing more clearly than ever before, I'd like to take a minute to explain what I mean by "cyberbullying," in a scientific way. Forgive me for the nerd lingo, but I think it's necessary to fully understand this emerging field.

CYBERBULLYING—A RETROSPECTIVE

Until now, I'd only just scratched the surface with the kind of cyberbullying I'd taken part in at the Organic School, using cell  phones and computers to terrorize kids who I know. Beyond this, there's an entire expansive realm of anonymous cyberbullying out there. I'm talking about the anonymous attacks I've been carrying out over the last few days where I do not know my victim, and they do not know me. Like a blind date where everything goes horribly. The important distinction being the anonymity of the relationship between bully and bullied.

Before launching into the various manifestations of this kind of anonymous cyberbullying, it's important to first understand the underlying premise of all cyberbullying—that people put things online that they should not. Pictures, videos, status updates, private thoughts, and journal entries—shared with the entire world for no good reason. This creates an opening for the cyberbully to abuse this overshare of information for personal, destructive gain.

That, in combination with the sweet, sweet anonymity of the Internet, is the perfect storm for the cyberbully hurricane.

Some of my favorite new cyberbullying techniques include:

Trolling—this is when you go onto other people's blogs, Facebook, or Twitter and leave mean comments specifically designed to upset. Some good generic trolls include "you = stupid," "this is the dumbest thing in the world, did you overdose on dumb pills this morning?" and "sucktastic." TRY TYPING IN ALL CAPS TO SHOW YOU REALLY MEAN BUSINESS.

Advanced Trolling—this is trolling specifically reserved for YouTube and other video sites. These are cesspools full to the brim with trolls, so your comments have to be extra cutting and hurtful in order to make the cut. One that I find often does the trick, for example, on a fifteen-second-long video, is to write "worst fifteen seconds of my life. I want them back." TYPE IT IN CAPS IF YOU REALLY MEAN IT.

Cyber Harassment—get someone's e-mail address and send them angry messages. I like to call kids fat and smelly, as that is a problem I myself deal with and it feels good to project those feelings of despair onto others. Shatner would be so proud.

Video Remixing—for experienced cyberbullies only. This is when you take a regrettable video someone posted online, showing them doing something stupid, and remix it into an ultra-catchy bass beat so people can't resist sending it to everybody they know.

Girl Cries About Losing Beauty Pageant — Niko DUbsTeP remix

"It's just not fair!
Just not just not fair!
The other girls
They were so mean!
I should be queen!
I should I should be
q-q-q-q-queen!"

Collecting Insurance—anytime someone posts a pic of themselves doing something idiotic, just save a copy to your computer. E-mail it to the person who posted it a year or two years or even ten years later asking for money to keep it under wraps.

That's all for now. I've got more work to do.

Sunday

Took a quick thirty-minute nap because Mom said
I had to. She just doesn't understand that the
Internet never sleeps! I've got work to do and she's
throwing a wrench in my gears. I'll have to send her
some mean anonymous e-mails.

Anyway, Alex came into my room today to see if I
wanted to take MurderZombie on a walk. As if I care
about that wimpy dog anymore! I normally would have
just kicked them both out, but something inside of
me—maybe it was my urge to brag or just being locked
in my room for four days—drove me to invite them in
and share my newfound talent.

Yo, Alex—come here! You've got to check this out!

I was about five minutes into my explanations of the manifestations of cyberbullying and their real-world applications, when Alex stopped me.

I had so much to say I talked for almost twenty minutes! Afterward, I crashed hard. The Internet might not need sleep, but cyberbullies do.

Monday

After waking up in a great mood, albeit a little tired, I decided to log on for the hour before school and see what the world's nerds had posted on YouTube, then leave mean-spirited comments to the order of:

"You stink. Go suck a puke booger, loser face."

Or:

"Laaaaaaaaame. Were you born that dumb, or do you train for it?"

Or, if I'm feeling particularly hurtful:

"You are what's wrong with the world. Do everyone a favor and LEAVE!!!!!!!"

Well, I was in for a treat, because the number-one most watched video had a particularly intriguing title that scratched me right where I itched.

Fat, nerdy computer geek humiliates self.

40,012,291 views

puppy + trampoline = fun

21,229,821 views

lady has a bikini

7,292,885 views

I clicked the link and watched all twenty minutes, but did not laugh once. It seems Alex had been recording me while I pattered away about all my cyber exploits. They sounded a whole lot nerdier now that I listened to them out loud.

The coolest thing about the Internet is how it connects you to other people, like a mystical friendship web made of rainbows and spiders!

After being online only a few hours, this thing had already been seen by most of the country and soon to be world. It was more disgustingly viral than Grandpa's back shingles.

And that was only the tip of the iceberg. My video had more comments than the "fat guy marries pizza" video, and they weren't nearly as nice.

The top three upvoted comments were as follows:

"HAHA! This guy is the most pathetic nerd I've ever seen."
— buttfartz6969

"Too funny. He's even fatter than that guy who married the pizza."
— /ady_on_the_net80085

"This guy is what's wrong with the world. LEAVE!!!!!"
— MegaMan21

I exploded into Alex's room like a fusion bomb and demanded that he take down the video.

This is what you get for destroying my robot statue. I told you I'd get you back.

Take it down or I'll do to you what I did to that stupid robot!

He caved pretty fast. It was no use though. As soon as he removed it, thirty new copies of the video sprang up in its place, complete with techno rap remixes.

Biggest Geek on Planet rap remix

Cyber bullies are online trolls,
like a cyber highway
with with with bully tolls
mani-mani-manifestations!

There's no stopping this. I've seen it go down a million times. So I did the only thing I could do: record a retaliation video to shut up all those blog-o-geeks out there.

Shut the heck up, Internet! You should know that I've alerted the local police AND the cyber police. If you don't stop trolling my video, the consequences will never be the same!!!

I should have realized from the many videos I have laughed at and commented on this weekend, that this would only add to my problems.

Whiny Baby Cries at Internet RAP REMIX

My life is over.

Tuesday

When I realized there's no way to remove all the videos, I kinda freaked out and had a breakdown. Mom came in to take me to school and I lost it. I cried for a couple hours and couldn't stop shaking. Mom called Dr. Shatner, who told her to keep me home and bring me in later this week.

Ok, Dr. Shatner, he'll rest up and we'll see you Wednesday.

NOT LOOKING FORWARD TO THAT. YOU CAN TELL BY MY CAPS THAT I MEAN IT TOO.

I've had to go into hiding. I've deleted all my web accounts. I even got rid of my Twitter comedy account, "Dumb Stuff My Mom Thinks," which had been optioned by NBC Universal for a trilogy of trilogies.

To make matters worse, the web geeks somehow figured out my name, so if you Google "Niko Kayler" you get a thousand pages of people ragging on me and calling me horrible names. My real world was already wrecked. Now, thanks to Alex, my online world is gone too. I don't know what to do. I'm sick to my stomach. I wish I had a secret bunker in Pakistan to retreat to.

WEDNESDAY

At our weekly therapy session, I think Shatner could tell something was wrong.

This is the lowest I've ever felt. I actually find myself wishing I was back at the Reform School, getting pummeled by Brittany Flowers and her drones. Getting punched in the face and flushed down the toilet would feel better than this.

Shatner kept asking if I felt well enough to go back to school. Are you kidding me? I don't think I'll ever be able to go back. What's worse—it's not just the Organic School for Local Kids— every middle school kid on the planet has seen this thing. Even if I enrolled in a tiny school in Düsseldorf, they'd still know who I was.

Ich beende Ihren Kerl, Sie wimpy Baby. Ich bin Ihr führer!

Thursday

Another pointless day on Earth. The only thing I can do to pass the time is do homework. It's pathetic, I know, but I've already crossed every other line from bully to nerd, so why not this one. I also renounced my membership to the American Bully Association and burned the once sacred bully flag that used to fly in my backyard.

Bullies are blood in, blood out. They're probably going to come for me. So be it. What else do I have to lose?

I don't even know who I am anymore. What in the world am I going to do with myself? Maybe I should go to law school?

Objection your Honor, witness is a turtle-face cheese-breath. Anything he says is dumb.

That would involve me going back out into the world, which is thoroughly impossible at this point. No matter what I do, people are always going to recognize me from that stupid video, even fifty years from now.

Mom brought me some ice cream and said I would have to go to school next week no matter what. Why does it take so long to fade into obscurity!?

Saturday
Dad called me today, probably because Mom made him.

Hey Chief, Mom said you had a little incident with the computer machines. I've heard that's pretty hard on kids these days. When I was a kid, I got picked on too, and look at me now—CEO of my own business. I'm living the dream, and you can too. Don't let those kids bring you down, OK?

Despite his fumbling and old-man out-of-touchness, what he said kind of helped.

He was so close. So close to doing something that actually helped, then he lit the frigging oil tanker on fire. Parents are pathetic.

Sunday

It had been a full week since the video went up and I was starting to feel a tiny, itty bitty bit better—not good, but I felt like I could breathe and think for a second. It was beginning to dawn on me that maybe cyberbullying was not as victimless a crime as I had first thought. Maybe this kind of anonymous tech-torture really did do bad damage to kids.

It's not so bad when the bully flow chart operates like this:

But sometimes, the flow is reversed, and happens to go more like this:

I guess this whole time I only saw things from one perspective. Dr. Shatner always told me to "think before I act," but I didn't listen.

Just then, Alex came into my room. Most of the time, if he pissed me off, I'd just scream and chase him out, but I think I've lost my will to bully.

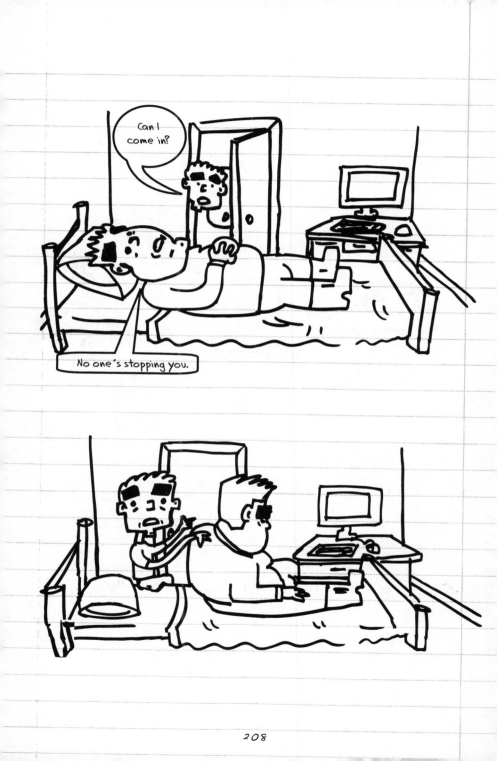

"Listen, Niko. I'm really sorry about posting that video."

"Yeah, right. I bet Mom is making you say that."

"No, I'm serious. I feel terrible."

"Really?"

"I just wanted to get you back for being a jerk and smashing my robot. That thing took me like a year to paint and glue together and you just smashed it like it was nothing."

"Well, at least there's not a video of that with two hundred million views to document the event for all eternity."

"Jeez, I said I'm sorry."

"It's probably beaming its way out into space as we speak. Somewhere there's an alien laughing so hard he shoots space milk out his spaktizorum."

"I don't know what else to say—I'm really sorry."

"Is sorry going to take my fat away?"

"What? Look—bad stuff happens. We moved here, away from all my friends and everything that mattered to me in the world. I was already feeling terrible, and then you decided to be a total butthead and texted the friends that I did have so they wouldn't be my friends anymore. I was completely alone, but you know what?"

"What?"

"Things got better. I kept going even when I was feeling absolutely awful and, in time, things got better."

"How did you do it?"

"When you are at rock bottom, you have nothing else to lose. I had no friends, no robot, no one I would call 'brother.' What else could they take from me? The only way to go was up."

"What do you mean?"

"I got an awesome puppy, joined a ballet class, and learned to bake. Now I have lots of friends and fun things to do. I'm never sad or lonely anymore. Except when I have done something stupid to my brother."

"I saw you in the park on Halloween. It did seem like you had a lot of new friends, but aren't puppies, ballet, and baking all stuff for girls?"

TEXT LOG

Ashlynn—let's hang 2nite
Brooke—you were so funny in ballet this week. ttyl
Isis—bffs?
Taylor—is Isis trying to steal you from me. That witch!
Eva—thinkin bout u
Angelina—do you have a GF??? Doesn't matter. I still want to hang out
Rachel—I think I love you
Starr—let's party ;)

"Exactly—I'm basically the only dude in ballet, and ladies love puppies and muffins. I do it just to meet girls. Check out the text log on my phone."

I don't know...it seems kinda...gay.

Do I need to grab you a dictionary?

After a brief consultation with this "dictionary" thing, it dawned on me—my little brother is a total and complete ladies' man.

I was starting to realize Alex might have a point.

"Dude—I think you may be on to something."

"Of course I am, Niko."

"I am at my rock bottom. What else can they do to me?"

"Nothing!"

"Do I have any dignity left to lose?"

"Not a drop!"

"Could I possibly feel any worse than I already do at this very pathetic moment?"

"Absolutely not!"

"I'm invincible."

"Precisely."

If you had told me that when we moved to Boulder that Alex would become some kind of know-it-all philosopher ladies' man, I would have laughed in your face and then punched you, but there it was right in front of me. What's more, he's right. The entire world is already laughing at me. How is going back to school going to make that any worse? Sure they'll snicker and point, but I've got nothing left to lose. I'm invincible.

Alex patted me on the back and then, very unexpectedly, punched me in the gut.

Alex went to bed, but left me with MurderZombie, who I guess at this point I should just cave and call SugarTummy. Ick!

Sitting there, staring at that adorable little goober, I was feeling pretty OK. Then I heard the familiar chime of a new message in my inbox.

Message from: Hillary Corrigan

Hiya Fatty,

Hope you are doing fat (I'm sure you are). Well, I was rotting away at
this sunny rehab clinic—thanks so much for that one, btw—and I happened to get forwarded a link. Apparently you've been busy making
internet videos of yourself. You're a celebrity! Do you know that the
web is calling you "The Fattest Nerd Alive"? I made you this decal you
can print off and put on a shirt so everyone will know it's you (like
they don't already)! Anyway, love ya!

Kisses,
Hill

At this point, all of the bad feelings that Alex had helped to soothe away came surging back. That hell spawn, Hillary! She knew exactly how to get at me. I sat there staring at SugarTummy trying to figure out what to do, and then it hit me.

I had spent dozens of hours trying to turn this tiny, happy-go-lucky pup into a killing machine. Dozens of hours, for nothing. Nothing I did or said or forced this puppy to watch could make it anything other than what it was deep down—an adorable free-spirited little pup.

A lot has happened to me this past week. I went from crowned king of the bullies, to a wimpy pile of tears. Am I going to let Hillary Corrigan make me something I'm not, am I gonna let her decide who I am, or am I going to stand up and be who I am deep down?

Monday

Haters gonna hate. And you know what? Let 'em.

I've taken some lickings this year—and not undeservedly. I'll think twice next time before I strike, but believe you me—this isn't over. Nobody is gonna tell me who I am!

By the end of this school year, I'll be on top again. I'll walk down these halls like this every freaking day, like my butt weighs a million pounds. Maybe I'll even take a page from Alex, and use this little dog to win over some ladies.

Yep, I'm gonna terrorize these—pardon my French—these mofos. I'm going to show them the world's greatest bully. That's who I really am, and that's who I'm going to be. When I'm done with these feel-good, new age punks they're going to join the army just to get to a more forgiving place.

Cyberbully out. For now.

Farley Katz lives in New York where he cartoons for *The New Yorker* magazine.

A fun and hilarious look at the bully's point of view.

Full of wedgies, wet willies, and wicked fun.

St. Martin's Griffin